GRIDIRON
SHOWDOWN

BY JAKE MADDOX

text by
Eric Stevens

STONE ARCH BOOKS
a capstone imprint

Jake Maddox JV books are published by Stone Arch Books
A Capstone Imprint
1710 Roe Crest Drive
North Mankato, Minnesota 56003
www.capstonepub.com

Library of Congress Cataloging-in-Publication Data

Maddox, Jake, author.
  Gridiron showdown / by Jake Maddox ; text by Eric Stevens ; illustrated by Mike Ray.
    pages cm. -- (Jake Maddox JV)
  Summary: Jasper quit his school football team after blowing a big play, which is giving him
a lot of time to get into trouble with his friends--but when he is allowed to rejoin the team
rather than face detention he finds that everybody is mad at him: his teammates because he
quit, and his friends because he is avoiding punishment.
  ISBN 978-1-4342-9155-4 (library binding) -- ISBN 978-1-4342-9159-2 (pbk.)-- ISBN 978-1-4965-
0066-3 (eBook PDF)
1. Football stories. 2. Friendship--Juvenile fiction. 3. Responsibility--Juvenile fiction.
4. Teamwork (Sports)--Juvenile fiction. [1. Football--Fiction. 2. Friendship--Fiction. 3.
Responsibility--Fiction. 4. Teamwork (Sports)--Fiction.] I. Stevens, Eric, 1974- author. II. Ray,
Mike (Illustrator), illustrator. III. Title.

  PZ7.M25643Gs 2014
  813.6--dc23

                                    2013047037

Art Director: Heather Kindseth
Designer: Veronica Scott
Production Specialist: Jennifer Walker

Photo Credits:
Shutterstock: Christina Loehr, cover 1; Dean Harty, chapter openings
Design Elements: Shutterstock

Printed in China by Nordica
0414/CA21400620
032014   008095NORDF14

TABLE OF CONTENTS

CHAPTER 1

BUSTED

Jasper Biggs grinned and looked around from his hiding spot beneath the football bleachers. Then he slowly pulled a lighter out of his pocket.

"Where did you get that?" his friend Charlene, whom everyone called Charlie, whispered.

Jasper and Charlie had grown up on the same street and had been friends since preschool. Now that they were in eighth grade, they'd become best friends, especially since Jasper had quit the football team last year. It meant he was around a lot more.

"He probably grabbed it from the shed," Jasper's other good friend, Anton, said as he snatched the lighter out of Jasper's hand. "It's the one his dad uses for the grill."

"Guilty," said Jasper, grabbing the lighter back. He pulled a packet of firecrackers out of his other pocket. "And these were hidden in the back of the garage for next summer."

"Whoa!" said Charlie. "Let's light them off!"

Jasper rolled his eyes. "Obviously," he said. "That's why we're here. We just have to wait for the right moment."

Jasper placed a couple of firecrackers on the dirt in front of them and squinted between the bleachers. On the field, the football team was practicing. The school year had just started, and it was the first year Jasper wasn't on the team.

"When will it be the right moment?" Charlie asked. "After your football buddies are done smashing into each other and playing with a ball?"

"They're not my buddies," Jasper snapped.

But the truth was, some of them were his friends — or at least they used to be. Back before Jasper had quit the team at the end of last season, he'd been best friends with some of the guys on the field. But then he'd blown a major play. That'd been the end of his football career.

"Besides," Jasper continued, "we don't have to wait for them to finish."

"You wouldn't dare set one off while they're practicing," Anton said. "Coach would kill you."

"I have to wait for the right moment," Jasper said again, still watching the team.

"Yeah, right," Charlie said, elbowing Anton. "I think you miss your old friends. That's why you're really down here — you want to watch them play."

Jasper didn't answer. He just watched as the football players practiced running plays. When they were finally done with the last drill, Coach blew his whistle.

Jasper had played football long enough to know that Coach loved to blow that whistle at the end of drills. It was the perfect opportunity.

"Now," Jasper whispered. He lit the firecrackers, and he and his friends hurried a few feet away. They watched as the firecrackers sparked across the dirt, banging and popping.

The plan worked great — Coach didn't notice the firecrackers exploding fifty yards away. *That whistle is so loud, he wouldn't notice if they were going off at his feet*, Jasper thought.

"Uh-oh," Charlie suddenly said. She pointed at the field. "Coach missed your little show, but it looks like a few of your old buddies noticed."

Jasper glanced over. Charlie was right. A few of the football players were elbowing each other and pointing right at Jasper, Anton, and Charlie. Any second now, even Coach — totally clueless about anything going on off the field — would notice.

"We'd better get out of here," Anton said.

The three of them shuffled along the dirt to the back of the bleachers. As soon as they were clear, they ran. But it was too late. Four members of the football team — looking huge in their uniforms with full pads and helmets — blocked them.

"Coach!" one of the boys yelled. Jasper recognized him as Kyle Jump, the team's starting running back this season. Last season, that'd been Jasper's position. Until he'd quit the team, that is.

"These jerks were setting off firecrackers," Kyle shouted, glaring right at Jasper.

Jasper turned and saw his former coach stomping toward them. The coach came around behind the bleachers and stood next to his four players. He was way bigger and tougher-looking than any of them, even in their uniforms.

Coach crossed his arms over his chest and glared at Jasper, Charlie, and Anton. "You three are coming with me," he growled. His voice was low and deep and angry. "Principal's office. Now."

CHAPTER 2

AN UNWELCOME SUGGESTION

"I'm getting a little tired of seeing you three," Principal Slate said a few minutes later. She peered over the top of her huge metal desk at the three kids on the other side. "You are quickly becoming the students I see in here the most."

The principal looked from Charlie to Anton to Jasper. "First it was your names in black marker on the lockers," she continued. "Then it was picking on sixth graders in the cafeteria. You've cut classes, left campus, and even let the air out of Mr. Herbach's electric car's tires."

"No one ever proved that was us," Charlie pointed out.

Principal Slate ignored her. "And now," she said, "I'm told you're shooting off illegal firecrackers on school grounds during football practice?"

As she stood there, with the afternoon sun coming in through the blinds behind her, the principal seemed to only look at Jasper. "I've tried the lectures," she went on. "I've tried keeping you three separated as often as possible, but you just clomp together as soon as the last buzzer rings."

Jasper looked at his two friends. They all shrugged.

"So what do we have left?" Principal Slate said. "Suspension?"

Anton and Charlie laughed, and the principal just shook her head. "No, you'd love that," she said. "I think we'll plan on this instead — two weeks of detention with Mr. Harrison."

"Ugh," Jasper said, letting his head roll back. Mr. Harrison had a reputation for being the sternest and meanest teacher at Pike Creek Middle School.

"I'm sure you'll all get along great with Mr. Harrison," Principal Slate said. She walked around from behind her desk and led the three of them to the door. "And since you'll be spending every moment you're not in class with him, you'll have plenty of time to get to know each other very well."

"Every moment?" Charlie repeated in horror as Principal Slate edged her toward the office door.

"That's right," said the principal. "That means he's your new homeroom teacher, your new lunch teacher, and your new study hall monitor. And of course he'll be with you from the time the last bell rings till the late bus leaves at four o'clock."

Anton and Charlie groaned as they walked out the door. Jasper moved to follow them, but Principal Slate grabbed him by the elbow before he could leave. "Just a minute, Jasper," she said. "I'd like to speak to you about something before you head home."

"Um, okay," he said. Charlie and Anton looked at him as the door closed, their eyes wide and a little afraid for him. "Am I in extra trouble?"

"It's nothing like that," said the principal. "I just have an idea for you. Charlene and Anton don't have any interests I know about, aside from starting trouble in my school and hanging out with you, that is. But you love football, isn't that right?"

Jasper shrugged. "I guess so," he said. He really did. He'd still be on the team if not for one very bad game last season.

"Good," Principal Slate said. "Then join the team again."

"What?" Jasper said.

As much as he still loved football, Jasper knew rejoining the football team was a very bad idea. After the way he'd screwed up last season, no one wanted him on the team again, including him. He'd blown a major play, and while he'd missed the team when he quit, it was for the best. For everyone.

"I think it would be great for you to have a positive activity to release some of that youthful energy," the principal went on. "Practice starts every day at four, so you'll be able to go after detention. And I expect your behavior will be back the way we all want it before long. I wouldn't be surprised if your grades went up, too."

"Are you saying I have to join the team?" Jasper asked.

"Of course not," said Principal Slate. "I'm merely suggesting you join." She leaned closer to Jasper, and her voice became even more serious as she said, "Strongly suggesting."

CHAPTER 3

DOING THE TIME

The next afternoon, Jasper and his friends got to know Mr. Harrison just as well as Principal Slate had threatened. And he was every bit as strict as Jasper had heard.

As soon as Jasper, Charlie, and Anton walked into his classroom, Mr. Harrison glared at them. "Welcome to the longest detention of your lives," he said through his teeth. "There will be no talking, no moving out of your seats, and no eye contact between the three of you at all. Got it?"

Detention went until four o'clock, and Mr. Harrison refused to release them even a moment early. When he finally let them go, he dismissed them in alphabetical order. None of them were allowed to talk until they were far enough away from his room that he wouldn't hear them.

"I'll see you three for homeroom tomorrow," Mr. Harrison said, locking the door behind them.

"Can't wait," Charlie muttered.

"I hope he didn't hear that," Anton replied when they were well down the hallway.

Jasper nodded. "He probably did," he said.

The three walked toward the main exit, but when they crossed the front hall, Jasper stopped. "I'm going this way," he said. He thumbed down the hall toward the locker rooms.

"The late bus is this way, bro," said Anton.

Jasper looked down at his feet, avoiding his friends' eyes. He hadn't told either of them he'd joined the football team again. "I know. But I have practice now," he said.

"You gotta be kidding me," Charlie said.

"Practice?" Anton said, looking confused. "What are you talking about?"

"Don't you get it?" said Charlie. She elbowed Anton but kept her eyes on Jasper. "Our friend here has rejoined the football team. That's why Slate held him back after the meeting."

Jasper shrugged.

"Is she giving you a break from detention if you join?" Charlie asked. She took an angry step toward Jasper.

"Nope," said Jasper.

"Then why are you joining?" said Anton.

Jasper shrugged again. He didn't want to admit to his friends that there was a little part of him that *wanted* to rejoin the team.

"Whatever," said Charlie, looking disgusted. She turned around and headed for the exit. "Come on, Anton," she called. "Let him get to practice."

With a final dirty look, Anton shook his head at Jasper and hurried after Charlie.

CHAPTER 4

CLEAN SLATE?

"Well, well, well," said Kyle Jump, Jasper's former teammate, as Jasper opened his cubby in the locker room a few minutes later. "If it isn't Jasper Biggs."

Jasper didn't reply. He just pulled his gym clothes out of his locker.

"Better known as Mr. Choke of last season," Kyle said. He was talking much louder now — loud enough that everyone in the locker room getting ready for practice could hear him. A few of the other teammates chuckled.

On the other side of the locker room, a door slammed shut. Jasper recognized the sound right away — Coach's office door.

As if on cue, Coach stomped into the locker room. He came to a stop when he reached Jasper and looked down at him with his arms crossed over his chest.

"Hi, Coach," said Jasper.

Coach bared his teeth. "You quit my team last year," he said. "You left us in the lurch because of one bad play."

Jasper almost laughed. *One bad play?* he thought. It had hardly been *one* bad play. He'd fumbled on a *key* play. If he'd scored, the team would have made the play-offs. But his mistake had cost them their spot. And that was the reason Jasper had quit.

"And now you're setting off firecrackers on my field during practice," Coach said.

"I'm sorry," Jasper said.

Coach stood up straighter and put a hand on Jasper's shoulder. "Clean slate right now," he said, his voice raspy and deep. "I'm glad you could make it today."

Jasper tried not to let his surprise show on his face. He'd expected his former coach to give him a much harder time.

"You'll see the rest of the team is already in uniform," Coach went on. "How about you arrive on time tomorrow so we don't have to wait?"

"Sorry, Coach," Jasper replied. "Again." He was about to add that his detention ended at four — the same time practice started — so it was impossible to get to practice on time. But he didn't have a chance. Coach blew his whistle sharply, making Jasper flinch and cover his ears.

Coach stuck his finger in his face. "On time," he said.

Jasper nodded. He wasn't sure the slate was quite as clean as Coach said.

Without another word, Coach turned and stomped toward the double doors that lead out to the football field. "Let's go, you bums!" he hollered at the rest of the team.

Kyle laughed as he jogged past Jasper, and his shoulder bumped him hard. "He means you," Jasper's replacement muttered.

Jasper shook his head and turned back to his locker to get ready. He didn't need to be any later.

"Jasper," a voice suddenly called from the other side of the lockers.

Even though it had been awhile since he'd heard it, Jasper recognized the voice at once. "Hey, Cole," Jasper called back.

Last season when Jasper had been the team's starting running back, Cole had been a starting guard. Cole was the biggest kid on the team. When he was blocking for Jasper, nothing stopped him.

Cole peeked around the lockers. "Don't let Kyle get to you," he said.

Jasper shrugged into his pads. "He's probably just mad he won't be getting the ball as much now that I'm back."

"Maybe," Cole said with a shrug. "Or maybe he's just a jerk."

Jasper smiled. He and Cole hurried after the rest of the team. All the other players were already gathered around Coach in the end zone.

"Let's show a little hustle, you two!" Coach called over the helmets of the rest of the team. Jasper and Cole jogged a little faster till they reached the group.

"Now, as many of you probably noticed," Coach said, "Jasper Biggs is back on the football team this year."

The team grumbled, and Kyle said, "Who invited him?"

"Principal Slate," Coach said, "and me. So keep your mouth shut on the matter, okay?"

Kyle grinned, but he didn't say anything else.

"Jasper, you probably already know Kyle has taken over as starting halfback," Coach said. "And we've got a starting fullback. I'm putting you on special teams."

Jasper's mouth fell open. "What?" he said. Normally he knew better than to talk back to Coach, but this was anything but normal. "But I'm a better runner than Kyle!"

"Right," said Kyle. "That's why you blew it on that run against Riverton last year, right?"

Jasper couldn't take it anymore. He pushed between his teammates and charged straight at Kyle. He knocked his shoulder right into Kyle's chest, and the boys fell to the grass, pulling and punching at each other.

Coach's whistle blew sharp and loud. Someone pulled Jasper up by the jersey. Kyle looked up at him, still grinning.

"If I see or hear anything else like this between you two today," Coach said, "or any day from here on out, you'll both be warming the bench till you graduate high school. Do I make myself clear?"

"Sorry, Coach," the boys muttered.

Coach gave them another hard look and blew his whistle again. Then he shouted, "Drills!"

CHAPTER 5

DON'T BLOW IT

When Jasper got home from practice that evening, he was starving. It had been a long time since he'd run that much. In fact, since quitting the team at the end of last year, he'd hardly done anything except hang out with Charlie and Anton. And they usually just played video games — not exactly a hard workout.

Jasper would have liked to sit right down for dinner. He could smell the lasagna, his favorite meal, baking in the oven. But apparently his mom had a different idea. "Jasper, can I talk to you in the living room for a minute?" she called. She didn't sound happy.

Jasper sighed and made his way into the living room. He took a seat on the couch and glanced up at his mother standing in front of him.

"Honey," his mom started, "I'm really glad you're back on the football team."

"You are?" Jasper said. He'd told his parents about rejoining the team — but not why he'd been forced to do it. "I thought you hated the football team. You always said you were afraid I'd get hurt all the time."

"And I still worry about that," Mom confessed. "But ever since you quit the team, you've been so miserable all the time. I think you've missed playing with your teammates."

"Maybe," said Jasper, wondering when he could eat.

"However," Mom said.

Jasper rolled his eyes. *Great, here comes the lecture*, he thought.

"I also got a call from your principal this morning," she said. "She told me you were caught playing with firecrackers?"

"Oh," Jasper muttered, avoiding his mom's gaze. "I was going to tell you . . ."

"And for that you're going to be punished," Mom finished just as Dad walked out into the living room.

"Isn't he already being punished?" Dad said. He dropped onto the couch beside Jasper. "They took away the firecrackers, right?"

"Yes," said Jasper, nodding.

"And you're getting loads of detention for two weeks?" Dad continued. "And are stuck in study hall and lunch and homeroom with that frightening Mr. Harrison?"

Jasper nodded again, and Dad shivered. "We met him during parent-teacher conferences last year," Dad said, glancing over at Mom. "He scared me, and I'm forty!"

Mom glared at him, but Jasper thought it was funny. He chuckled quietly.

"I'm just saying that maybe the school is punishing him enough," Dad finished. He smiled gently at Mom. "Maybe we can take it easy on the home front this time."

Mom sighed and crossed her arms. "Fine," she said. "We'll leave it at that. But I am disappointed in your behavior lately."

Mom turned and walked over to the kitchen. A moment later, Jasper heard the old oven clank open. Mom was being even less gentle with it than she usually was.

"Thanks," Jasper said quietly as he glanced over at his dad.

"Don't thank me," said Dad as he got to his feet. "I just said what I think is fair. But remember that you're getting a big second chance here,

Jasper. Both with the team and with getting in trouble in school. Most people never get a second chance. Don't blow it."

"Okay," Jasper said as his dad headed for the kitchen. "I won't."

CHAPTER 6

OUT OF PRACTICE

The next afternoon, Jasper was back in detention with Charlie and Anton. Thanks to Mr. Harrison's rules, they couldn't talk. That didn't stop Anton. He was trying to mouth something to Jasper — although it was hard to tell what he was saying — when Mr. Harrison caught him.

"Not a word, you two," Mr. Harrison said. "Not even silent words."

Jasper put his eyes back on his math book. He could hardly understand a thing on the page in front of him, but it gave him something to stare it.

At 3:55, Mr. Harrison got up from his desk. That was weird enough, since the man hardly moved — he was like a stone statue that could talk and see. But things got weirder still when he stepped up to Jasper's desk.

"Um," said Jasper. "Hello."

"You may leave detention," said Mr. Harrison. The words came out through his clenched teeth. His jaw was set like stone, and Jasper could tell the teacher wasn't happy.

Jasper glanced up at the clock on the wall. It was definitely not four o'clock yet. *Why is Mr. Harrison letting me out early?* Jasper wondered. *He's supposed to be the toughest teacher in school.*

"Principal Slate has asked me to dismiss you five minutes early," Mr. Harrison said in explanation. He glared at Jasper as he spoke. "I don't like it one bit, but apparently getting to football practice on time is more important than real and lasting discipline in this school."

Jasper was smart enough not to ask questions. He scooped up his bag, stuck his big math textbook under his arm, and hurried for the door.

As he reached the door, Jasper glanced back. Anton sat with his arms crossed, staring at the white board. Charlie squinted right at Jasper, her mouth twisted in an angry frown. It was clear that his two best friends weren't exactly happy for him.

* * *

Jasper was one of the first players on the field for practice. When Coach blew his whistle and shouted over the team's heads, Jasper was relieved that the coach was shouting at two other guys who were running late, rather than at him and Cole.

Coach started them off with drills. The boys ran wind sprints. They did a zig-zag fifty-yard-dash then shuffled side to side. By the time drills were over, Jasper was beat. His legs were sore, and his breath was short.

"Out of practice?" Cole asked.

Jasper nodded, trying to catch his breath. His breathing was fast and shallow after all the running. "A little," he finally managed to say. Jasper stood up straight and tried not to let on that he had a cramp in his side. "I can handle it."

Just then, Coach let loose a long shriek on his whistle. "Okay, men!" he hollered. "Let's have a quick scrimmage. Two fifteen-minute halves. No time-outs."

Coach started pointing at team members, calling out "yellow." The boys he pointed to went to the sidelines and began suiting up in yellow scrimmage jerseys.

"Coach," said Jasper, taking a step toward him. His breath was back now, and he kept his head high and confident. "Let me play running back for the scrimmage."

Coach glanced over at Kyle, who was already pulling on a yellow jersey. "All right," he agreed.

"Let's see what a year off means. Kyle, no jersey for now. Jasper will take a few running plays to start."

* * *

The yellow team kicked off first to start the scrimmage. Cole, who was playing on Jasper's team, caught the kick and ran it back to their own forty-yard line.

On the very first play, Paul Kalio, their quarterback, said to Jasper, "You're running. Come around on the right."

Jasper nodded. He was excited, but nervous. He hadn't taken a hand-off in a game since the final game he'd played last season. That time hadn't gone well.

Jasper lined up on the left. Before the snap, he dropped back and ran around behind Paul. The center passed the ball back to the quarterback, who quickly turned left and then right, slipping the ball into Jasper's arms as he ran past.

Jasper immediately turned up the field. The offensive line pressed against the defense, creating a hole for him to run through. Jasper found the gap and took off up field as fast as he could. With Cole providing solid blocks, Jasper had no problem slipping past the line.

Once he was past the defense, Jasper saw sixty yards of nearly open field in front of him. Only one thing stood between him and a touchdown — a cornerback, who'd left his receiver across the field when he saw it was a running play.

Jasper cut to the right and ran up the out-of-bounds line. He kept one eye on the cornerback as the other player came speeding toward him. At the last moment, Jasper spun to dodge the hit — but it didn't work. The cornerback plowed into Jasper, pushing him out of bounds and knocking the ball from his hand.

Jasper heard the whistle blow and a lot of hooting and cheering from the other guys on the team. His head spun, and his whole body hurt. The corner stood over him with his hand out. Jasper took it and let him pull him up. Then he got right in his opponent's face.

"You trying to kill me?" Jasper said.

"That was a legal hit," the corner said. "You're just mad your little spin didn't work."

Coach jogged over before a fight broke out. "Take it easy, Jasper," Coach said. "He's right. It was a legal hit. You're wearing your pads. It was a good run. Let it go."

Jasper glared at the cornerback for another long moment before turning and jogging back to his team's huddle.

The cornerback shouted after him, though. "You're out of practice, Choke!"

Cole patted Jasper on the back when he reached the huddle. "Don't worry about that," he said. "Nice run."

But Jasper hardly heard him.

CHAPTER 7

QUITTER

The next morning, Jasper stood at his open locker, digging through his backpack to find the math homework he was eighty percent sure he'd done. Charlie leaned on the closed locker next to him, watching him search.

"I know I did it," Jasper muttered as he dug.

"Well, you better hurry," Anton called from his position across the hall. He tossed a little blue rubber ball across the hall and caught it when it bounced back at him. "You know Mr. Harrison will be watching the clock. We can't be late."

Charlie glanced down at her plastic watch. "You have like ninety seconds," she told him.

Jasper rifled faster through the papers in his backpack. He'd never quite gotten the hang of putting handouts and worksheets in folders and notebooks like his teachers always wanted him to.

"Jasper," a voice called. Without looking up, Jasper could tell it was Cole. But he didn't reply. He was too focused on finding that homework.

"Sixty seconds," Charlie warned.

Cole walked over to Jasper. He reached out a hand and patted his shoulder. "Hey, Jasper," Cole said. "You did pretty well at practice yesterday."

"I guess," Jasper mumbled.

Relief washed through him as he spotted a paper that looked like his homework. "Here it is!" Jasper said, much louder, but then he groaned. "Nope. This is from last week."

"Thirty seconds!" Charlie urged, bouncing on her toes. "Hurry up!"

"Got it!" Jasper said, tugging a wrinkled sheet of paper from his bag. He quickly yanked out his math notebook and stuffed the worksheet inside.

"See you later, Jasper," Cole said as Jasper and his friends started off down the hallway.

"Look, Cole," Jasper said, stopping for an instant. He was all too aware of how little time they had to get to Mr. Harrison's homeroom. "I get that you're trying to be nice. But forget about it. I'm probably quitting the team anyway."

"What?" Cole said. "Why?"

"No one wants me there," Jasper said. "And I'm out of practice. Everyone says so."

"So what?" Cole said. "Isn't that the point of practice? Besides, the season hasn't even started yet. And I heard Principal Slate made you join. Doesn't that mean you can't quit?"

"She can't make me stay," Jasper said.

With that, Jasper hurried off with Charlie and Anton. Cole stomped away in the other direction.

CHAPTER 8

SPECIAL TEAMS BLUES

Despite what he'd told Cole, Jasper suited up and hit the football field later that afternoon. He stood with the rest of the special teams players just inside the end zone.

"Are you guys ready?" Jimmy Unger, the football team's only kicker, shouted from the fifty-yard line. Jasper and the other special teams players nodded.

"This is boring," Jasper mumbled. The other guys ignored him. Most of them were happy to be on the football team at all.

Jimmy pulled a ball from the sack on the ground next to him. He held it up, took a short approach, and punted it. He wasn't a bad kicker. Jasper ran about five yards out of the end zone, caught the kick, and ran it back to Jimmy.

"Nice catch," said Jimmy.

Jasper didn't answer. He just started walking back toward the end zone while Jimmy punted another ball to the next guy in line.

A whistle suddenly blasted from the sidelines. "Let's see a little hustle, Jasper!" Coach shouted.

Jasper obediently turned his walk into a jog. When he reached the front of the line again, Jimmy kicked the ball. This time, the punt came down close to the sideline at the ten-yard line. Jasper tried to get to it before it hit the turf, but he was too late. The ball bounced and flew end-over-end into the metal bleachers.

"Hustle, Jasper!" Coach shouted from the other side of the field.

Jasper crawled under the side of the bleachers and found the ball. It was in Charlie's hands. "Lose something?" his friend asked.

Anton, who was standing next to her, started cracking up.

"Oh, very funny, man," Jasper said. "Just give it here."

"Fine," Charlie said, tossing him the ball. "We're going to Anton's place to play Zombie Attack 3000. There's some new stuff to download. Enjoy practice."

Jasper watched Anton and Charlie walk away, and his shoulders sagged. He could tell his friends were mad at him, but he didn't know what to do about it.

And there's nothing I can do about it now, Jasper thought as he jogged out from under the bleachers. He tossed the football back to Jimmy before running back to the end zone to take another turn receiving.

The next punt came in like a wild helicopter, spinning madly and moving fast. Jasper sprinted out of the end zone toward the incoming kick. He managed to make it to the ten-yard line just as the ball dropped out of the air and into his open arms.

For a moment, everything was perfect. But then he bobbled it. The ball bounced out of his arms and off his fingertips before hitting the turf and rolling out of bounds.

Jasper stopped, dejected, and stared at the sky.

Coach blew his whistle again. "Three laps around the field, Jasper," he called. "Chop, chop."

Jasper sighed. He could hear Kyle and some of the new running backs on the offensive line laughing at him as he started his first lap. By the time he'd finished it, his legs were tired and his chest burned.

Cole came up alongside him, jogging with him. "Man, you never would have dropped that last year," he said. "What's going on?"

Jasper glared at him. "I told you, I'm out of practice. I'm no good anymore. That's why I need to quit the team."

"Nah," said Cole. He slowed to a walk to let Jasper finish his laps on his own. "That's why you need to practice."

Jasper jogged on, his face hot with frustration. *But I don't want to practice catching kicks and returning punts*, he thought. *I want to practice sweeps and tosses and draws — running back plays.*

CHAPTER 9

PROVE IT

That night, Jasper devoured his dinner, hardly looking up from his plate the whole time. He concentrated on shoveling chicken and potatoes into his mouth, ignoring the carrots and beans.

"You're awfully quiet tonight," Mom said. "Is everything okay?"

Jasper just shrugged, not saying a word.

"I wish you'd tell us what's got you so down," his mother said. She leaned her chin on her folded hands and squinted at Jasper. "Is everything okay at school?"

With a sigh, Jasper looked at his mom. Of course everything wasn't okay at school. Nothing had been okay since he'd been forced to rejoin the football team.

Jasper looked back down at his plate. Everything except the orange and green veggies was gone. "Can I go to my room now?" he asked. "I'm done."

"Oh, eat some vegetables," Mom said.

Jasper sighed again loudly.

"Fine, go ahead," Mom said.

Jasper pushed back his chair. *I wonder if Charlie and Anton are still online*, he thought as he hurried upstairs. *Maybe I can find them in Zombie Attack.*

In his bedroom, Jasper switched on his game console and downloaded the new game. He logged on and spotted Anton's and Charlie's usernames right away. He was just about to message them when there was a knock on his bedroom door.

"Jasper," said his dad through the door. "Open up. I want to talk to you."

Great, Jasper thought. *Just as I was about to start playing.* He tossed his controller aside, switched off the TV, and opened the door. "What?"

Dad gave him a stern look that clearly said he didn't care for Jasper's tone.

"Sorry," Jasper said. "I mean, what is it, Dad?"

Dad sighed. "Sit," he said. Jasper took a seat on the edge of his bed and stared at the ceiling. "Why don't you tell me what's bugging you."

"Nothing," Jasper said. He glanced at the game console's glowing blue light. His friends were probably trying to talk to him, but there was no way he could respond with Dad in his room.

Dad followed his gaze. "The game will still be there when we're done talking," he said, "and when you've done your homework."

Jasper sighed. "Look," he said. "I haven't told you yet because honestly I'm embarrassed."

"About what?" Dad asked.

"I'm stuck on special teams this season," Jasper said, finally meeting his father's eyes. "Coach is leaving Kyle in my old position."

"Ah," said Dad, nodding. He took a seat at Jasper's desk and crossed his arms. "Well, you did quit the team."

"I know," Jasper muttered. *Like I need to be reminded.*

"If I were Coach," Dad went on, "I wouldn't just hand Kyle's position back to you either. Not after you turned your back on the team."

"What?" Jasper exclaimed. He couldn't believe what he was hearing. "I didn't —"

Dad held up a hand to stop him. "I'm just saying that's how Coach might see it," he said, standing up. "And I bet that's how Kyle sees it too."

Jasper sighed and let his shoulders sag. He knew he'd messed up big time last season. That's why he'd quit.

But I didn't mean to turn my back on anyone, Jasper thought. *If anything, I figured the rest of the guys would be happy to have me gone.*

"I'm just saying," Dad said, standing in the open doorway, "if you can't respect the position you've been given for the good of the team, maybe you don't belong on the team at all."

Jasper shrugged.

"Or maybe you don't respect the team, the coach, or the school," Dad finished.

Jasper thought back to his talk with Principal Slate. She'd said he needed to show he cared, and his grades and behavior would follow. "Yes, I do," he said. At least, he *thought* he did. Maybe.

"Then prove it," Dad said. "Get back into shape and earn your spot on special teams."

With that Dad left Jasper's room, closing the door behind him. Jasper got up and turned off the game console. Suddenly he didn't much feel like defending a city from a zombie attack anymore.

CHAPTER 10

EARNING YOUR KEEP

On Saturday morning, Jasper woke up early. He was still the last one out of bed, but for once he was dressed — in sweats and his old team jersey — before Dad had even finished his coffee.

As Jasper came into the kitchen and poured himself a glass of juice, Dad hurried to the wall calendar. He frantically flipped through the months, scanning the dates.

"What are you doing?" Jasper said, looking confused.

"You're up before lunchtime," Dad said. "It must be Christmas morning, right?"

"Haha," Jasper said with a laugh, rolling his eyes. He drank his juice in one long gulp. "I'm just up early to get a few drills in out back, okay?"

"Okay with me," Dad said. He sat back down, sipped his coffee, and opened the newspaper.

Jasper rinsed his glass and headed outside. Mom was already outside and digging up half the yard. Her weeding tools lay in a pile on the grass. A big plastic garbage can, already half full of yard waste, stood in the middle of the path that ran to the garage.

"Um," Jasper said. "I guess I can't run drills."

"No," Mom said, jabbing at the ground with a little spade. "But you can help me clean up the yard if you want."

"No thanks," Jasper said. "I guess I'll call Cole."

Jasper knew his mom would love that. She had always liked Cole — unlike how she felt about Anton and Charlie. And he hadn't called Cole in a long time.

Before his mom could look up from the yard work — or rope him into helping her — Jasper hurried inside and grabbed the phone.

* * *

Cole lived in the neighborhood on the other side of the school, so the two boys agreed to meet at the football field. When Jasper arrived, Cole was already there lacing up his shoes. He'd brought a football too.

"Hey," said Jasper as he walked up. "Thanks for showing up."

"Sure," said Cole. He stood up and bounced on his toes to loosen up. "Want to practice some runs like last year?"

Jasper had almost forgotten. Back before he'd quit the team, he and Cole would often meet at the field on Saturday mornings to practice runs and blocks. Sometimes they would just throw the ball back and forth. Today, though, Jasper had something else in mind.

"Can you kick?" Jasper asked. He dropped to the grass to stretch a little.

"I can try," Cole said. "Does this mean you're not planning to quit?"

"Yup," said Jasper. He stood up and jogged to the far end zone.

"Even though you're still on special teams?" Cole asked. He held the ball at one end, with his hand wrapped around the laces.

"Just kick the thing already, will you?" Jasper hollered to his friend. It was a cool morning, so he blew into his hands to warm them up a little bit before catching.

"Here it comes!" Cole shouted. He took a couple of steps, pulled back, and kicked as hard as he could.

Cole wasn't a great punter, but he was a strong enough kicker to send the ball flying a good distance down the field, even if it wasn't a terribly accurate kick. Instead of heading straight toward

Jasper, the ball veered off toward the side of the football field.

Jasper ran toward the sideline, where the ball was coming down in a floppy spiral. He reached out at the last moment and nearly grabbed it with one hand.

Nearly. It bounced off his fingertips and rolled onto the track. Jasper quickly scooped it up and rocketed it back to Cole.

"Nice hustle," Cole called. "Ready for another?"

Jasper nodded as he jogged back to the end zone. *I'm out of practice*, he told himself. *So this is what it takes. Practice.*

CHAPTER 11

FRIENDLY COMPETITION?

On Monday afternoon, after yet another silent detention, Jasper ran into Cole on his way to the locker room for practice.

"How are you feeling?" Cole asked. He put out his fist, and Jasper bumped it with his own. "You probably haven't worked out that hard in a year."

"I'm actually feeling pretty good," Jasper said. He stretched his neck from side to side. "I bet Coach will see a difference today."

The boys pushed through the locker room doors and saw Kyle standing in front of them. It was almost as if he'd been waiting for them.

"Wow," Kyle said with a mean grin. "I can't believe you actually showed up."

"Stuff it, Kyle," said Cole. He pushed past his teammate and headed for his locker.

Jasper moved to follow, but Kyle stepped forward to block him.

"I thought you'd spend the whole weekend goofing off with your detention besties," Kyle said. "Maybe letting Charlie massage your sore legs?"

"Shut up, Kyle," Jasper said. He tried to get past Kyle again, but Kyle blocked him.

"Come on, Jasper," Kyle said, grinning. "With moves that predictable you'll never get your spot back." Then he laughed.

"Oh, yeah?" Jasper said. "How about this move?" He reached out with both hands and shoved Kyle in the shoulders.

Kyle fell backward, sprawling over a bench. He landed with a bang and thud against the metal lockers behind him.

Jasper was mad, but he immediately knew he'd done something pretty stupid. As if to confirm it, Coach's shrill whistle blasted through the locker room. Kyle sat up, embarrassed but unhurt, and glared at Jasper.

"What happened here?" Coach asked. He looked back and forth between Jasper and Kyle. Kyle stood up, but neither of the boys answered their coach.

"All right, you don't feel like explaining," Coach said. "Then get dressed. Full pads. You two are running laps together."

"What?!" Kyle exclaimed. "But that's not —"

"You two ready to tell me what happened?" Coach interrupted, taking a step toward the running back.

But Kyle stayed stubbornly silent, glaring at Jasper furiously.

"Okay then," Coach said. "A mile in pads. Get moving, boys."

The rest of the team had gathered now and stood around watching the scene unfold. Coach turned around and blew his whistle sharply. "The rest of you waiting for laps too?" he snapped.

Everyone, including Jasper and Kyle, hurried to get geared up. Cole hung back near Jasper.

"Bummer," Cole said as they went outside. "You think you can handle a mile in pads?"

Before Jasper could reply, Kyle jogged up behind them. "Him?" he said. "No way. He'll probably get tired halfway though and then quit the team — again."

With that, Kyle cackled and ran faster, up to the track to start the mile.

Coach, already up on the field, blew his whistle in Jasper's direction. "Hustle, Jasper," he said. "I don't want to see Kyle too far ahead."

"Good luck," Cole muttered.

Jasper nodded. Then he took off running in the direction of the track.

After the first lap, Jasper was feeling okay. His legs were still sore from yesterday, and he didn't remember his pads weighing quite so much, but he was keeping up with Kyle.

He let the running back stay a few yards ahead of him. That way he wouldn't be forced to run right side by side.

Kyle didn't look tired at all. His head was high, his elbows stayed sharp, and his legs pumped high on each stride.

"Can't keep up?" Kyle shouted back over his shoulder at Jasper. He kicked up a little more speed and widened the gap between them.

As Jasper reached the end of the second lap, Kyle was almost fifty yards ahead. Jasper put on a little more speed, trying to close that gap, but every time he did, Kyle seemed to move a little faster too.

As Kyle entered a straightaway on the third lap, Jasper rounded the curve and put on some speed, managing to close the distance — a little. He ran past the bleachers, vaguely aware of Coach's shouts and whistles from the football field inside the track.

As they came around the next curve and entered the fourth lap, Jasper forced himself to run even faster. He was within twenty-five yards of Kyle. In front of him, Kyle kicked up his speed too.

Jasper's legs burned with the effort. He gritted his teeth against the pain. As he got closer to Kyle, he could hear the other boy breathing fast and heavy. Now he was working hard, too.

I can catch him, Jasper thought.

They came to the last straightaway. The infield was silent — the whole team had noticed the impromptu race taking place on the track.

A hundred yards to go. Jasper pushed as hard as he could. He and Kyle were neck and neck.

But try as he might, Jasper couldn't push any harder. Kyle could, though.

With only fifty yards to go, Kyle put forth one final burst of speed. He crossed the finish line — a few steps ahead of Jasper.

"Nice going, Kyle," Coach said as both boys jogged into the infield.

Jasper wanted to collapse onto the grass, but somehow he managed to stay on his feet. With his hands on knees, he gasped for air, trying to catch his breath.

Beside him, Kyle did the same. Only Kyle was smiling and didn't seem to be struggling nearly as much as Jasper was.

The rest of the team followed Coach to the fifty-yard line for drills.

"Not bad, Jasper," Kyle said, straightening. He patted Jasper's shoulder pad. "Maybe you're not as out of practice as we thought." Then he jogged over to join the rest of the team.

CHAPTER 12

GAME DAY

The first real football game of the season was Thursday. It was a big day, but that didn't mean Jasper got a pass. He still had to join Charlie and Anton in detention. It was the only place he saw either of them lately.

They had a few minutes before the bell rang, and Mr. Harrison wasn't in the room, so Anton wasn't in his chair yet. Instead, he was leaning over Jasper's desk at the front of the room.

"I still can't believe you're going to play in the game today," Anton said, shaking his head. Across the room, Charlie sat on her own desk facing them, but she didn't say anything. She just watched.

"Leave me alone, Anton," Jasper muttered. He glanced up at the clock. Two more minutes until detention started.

"It just seems to me," Anton said as he pushed away from Jasper's desk, "that if I were you, I'd be pretty mad at the football coach."

"Why?" Jasper asked without looking at him.

Anton paced behind Jasper's chair. "Just think about it," he said. "You're the star running back. A kid who not only ran for a bazillion yards last season, but scored no fewer than seven hundred touchdowns."

"Oh, give it a rest," Jasper said. He glanced over at Charlie, who rolled her eyes.

"And yet here we are, the very next season," Anton went on as he hurried to stand between Jasper and Charlie, "and he's stuck you on specialties —"

"Special teams," Jasper put in.

"— returning punts and kicks like total a chump," Anton finished.

"You don't know a thing about football, do you?" Jasper snapped. He turned in his chair to watch as Anton went to take his seat at the back of the room.

"I know enough," Anton said.

"Oh, lay off," Charlie said. She smiled at Jasper and added, "I'm proud of him."

At her words, Jasper felt his whole face getting hot — both with embarrassment and surprise.

Just then, the door flew open and the buzzer buzzed. Mr. Harrison took his seat at the front of the room and knocked twice on the table with his knuckles — his signal for, "Shut up, sit down, and do some work." So they did.

CHAPTER 13

TEAM EFFORT

Pine Creek won the coin toss that afternoon, which meant the team from Green Mountain Junior High would kick off to start the game.

Cole took the field as upback — a second-string running back who could block. Jasper hurried up behind him to return the kick.

"Feeling good?" Cole asked as they jogged to the twenty-yard line.

"Not bad," Jasper said.

The kick-return team took their positions in a wedge. At the other end of the field, the Green

Mountain kicker lifted his arm and approached the football. He picked up speed and cut upfield as he kicked the ball.

The ball shot toward Pine Creek's team and came down near the sideline just inside the fifteen-yard line. Jasper scooped it up after one bounce. He looked upfield and saw the Green Mountain team bearing down on him.

Cole cleared a path for him, and Jasper took it. He had some open grass now, but not for long. Four Green Mountain defenders stood between him and the thirty. Jasper juked and lost two of the defenders, but the others wrapped him up and brought him down.

Some of his teammates patted Jasper on the helmet as he jogged to the bench. It wasn't a bad return, but it wasn't great. And now he'd be stuck on the bench watching Kyle play.

Kyle got up from the bench as Jasper sat down and pulled off his helmet. "Hey," Jasper said.

"Good luck out there." He put out his fist. Kyle bumped it and nodded. Then he pulled on his helmet and hurried out to the huddle.

Kyle's first play had him taking a hand-off and running behind the line toward the left side. He cut upfield as the defense collapsed onto him. He spun twice and managed a gain of six yards.

As Jasper watched from the bench, he could almost feel the football in his arms and the crunch of two tackles knocking him out of bounds. *I just want to get out there and play*, he thought.

Practicing and getting back in shape had been tough, but it had also made him realize that he really had missed football.

Out on the field, Pine Creek converted twice, but they only managed to get within field goal range and scored the three points. On Green Mountain's next possession, though, the Pine Creek defense held them behind their own twenty. On fourth down, they had to punt.

Cole, Jasper, and the rest of the kick-return team jogged out to the field and lined up near their forty-yard line. Three Pine Creek players lined up closer to the line of scrimmage, just in case the other team faked the punt.

The Green Mountain punter called for the snap and kicked. The ball flew high in the air, end-over-end, and right into Jasper's arms. But the wobbly flight made it tricky to catch, and the ball bounced up from his arms.

Jasper managed to grab the ball with one hand before it got away from him. He pulled it tightly into his chest as Cole took out one defender, then another that was speeding toward Jasper.

Jasper juked toward the sideline and then sprinted into midfield, where the grass was wide open. Ahead, Cole pushed back on two defenders as the defensive line rushed toward Jasper.

Jasper ran clear across the field toward the left sideline, pulling the gang of defenders with him. He had the speed, though, and he cut upfield, sprinting along the sideline with Cole at his side.

When he crossed the fifty-yard line, the crowd started to cheer. Out of the corner of his eye, Jasper could see the defense closing in on him. But he could see something else too — his teammates jumping up from the bench and cheering him on.

As he crossed the forty-yard line, a defender dove for his legs. Jasper leapt over his outstretched arms. Next to him, Cole stopped a defender with a perfect block. Jasper spun to dodge the Green Mountain center, a big slow guy who could have crushed him. But he had to catch him first.

The end zone was getting closer. Jasper crossed the thirty. Only the punter stood between him and six points. As he sprinted past the metal bleachers, Jasper saw his parents standing in the front row, clapping and cheering.

Behind his mom and dad, crouched under the seats as usual, were Charlie and Anton. Jasper grinned when he realized even his friends were cheering.

As Jasper crossed the twenty, the opposing punter dove at him and caught him by the foot. Cole had to jump to avoid stomping on the punter's torso.

But Jasper didn't give up, even with the punter's hands wrapped around his ankle and the rest of the defense rushing toward him. He pulled the punter right along with him, twisting and hopping, until the kicker finally shook loose.

Jasper put on an extra burst of speed, the football tucked high under one arm, and sprinted into the end zone for a touchdown.

The crowd went wild. Pine Creek's special teams members crowded around Jasper, patting his helmet and high fiving him.

"Nice blocks!" Jasper called to Cole, throwing an arm around his friend.

"Nice run!" Cole replied.

Back at the bench, Coach stepped up to Jasper. "We're going for two points on the conversion," he said, "and you're running it."

Jasper grinned. "Thanks, Coach," he said. He glanced over at Kyle, who stood at the bench.

Kyle looked at him and nodded quickly. Jasper nodded back and hurried out to the field to line up.

"I guess you made a good impression," Cole said at the line.

"Better not blow it," Jasper said.

"Don't worry," Cole said. "I'll get you through."

The quarterback called for the snap, faked to the left, and then turned and pressed the ball into Jasper's chest as he ran up. Jasper cut to the right, came around from behind the line, and pushed up the sideline with Cole flanking on the inside.

Jasper cut away from the sideline at the two. He launched himself over Cole and two defenders at the line. When he landed, his hand was outstretched into the end zone for two points.

CHAPTER 14

BACK ON THE TEAM

Pine Creek kept their lead the rest of the game. When the clock reached zero, they'd won, 15-10.

In the locker room, the whole team was celebrating. Coach blew his whistle to quiet everyone down.

"Good way to start the season, guys," Coach said. He crossed his arms high up on his chest and looked right at Jasper. "But I don't want to see anyone getting cocky."

Jasper nodded in understanding.

"We've all worked hard," Coach continued, "and we have a long season with a lot more hard work ahead of us. Not a single person on this team is more important than any other."

"Yes, Coach," the team said together.

"All right," Coach said. "Get showered and get out of here. No practice tomorrow."

As the team headed off to the showers, Kyle stepped up to Jasper. His lips were pressed in a tight line, and his hands were clenched into fists.

He's probably mad because Coach let me take that two-point conversion run, Jasper thought. "You going to fight me?" he asked.

"No," Kyle said, shaking his head. "I just wanted to say you ran well today. Better than me."

Jasper shook his head. "You ran for more than a hundred yards today," he protested.

"None of it was long gains," Kyle said. "Short bursts. No one cares about a five-yard gain here and a three-yard gain there."

"That's the job," Jasper said. "I got a lucky run. If I'd been in your position, it would have been the same for me. And if you'd been returning kicks, you could've gotten through for a touchdown."

"Maybe," Kyle said.

"It doesn't matter," Jasper said. "You're starting running back. I'm on special teams."

Kyle scoffed. "Yeah, for now," he said.

But Jasper wasn't done. He grabbed Kyle's shoulder. "No," he said. "For good."

* * *

Jasper spent Saturday and Sunday down at the football field, running drills with Cole and Kyle. By Monday, he was sore and tired, but he was also excited to get out to the field with the team again.

He was even more excited that his detention was finally over. After the last buzzer, he, Charlie, and Anton headed toward the exit.

"Are we ever going to see you again?" Charlie asked. "Now that detention is over, I mean."

"We still have class together," Jasper said. "And I'll be online to play Zombie Attack 3000."

"Haha," said Charlie, elbowing him lightly. "How about in real life?"

Jasper shrugged. "I won't be sneaking around with firecrackers and lighters anymore," he said. "I hope you'll keep coming to the games, though."

"Of course," Charlie said. She grinned at Jasper. "See you tomorrow." Then she headed for the exit. "Coming, Anton?"

"Um, yeah," Anton called. "Just a second."

Charlie shot him a quizzical look. Then she went outside to wait.

"Listen, Jasper," Anton said. "I have kind of a ridiculous question."

"What is it?" Jasper said.

"I was just thinking," Anton said. "My grades aren't so good. I get in trouble in class a lot."

"Yeah, you do," said Jasper with a chuckle.

"I'll probably be back in Harrison's detention class before too long," Anton went on.

"Without me," Jasper said.

"So, I was thinking," Anton said, looking down. "If I talk to Principal Slate first, do you think . . ."

"What?" Jasper asked.

"Do you think Coach would let me try out for the football team?" Anton finished quickly.

Jasper laughed. "Are you serious?" he said.

"Well, it worked for you, right?" Anton said. "Staying out of trouble and everything. Even Mr. Harrison likes you."

"You don't like football," Jasper said. "You don't know the first thing about football!"

"I can learn!" Anton insisted.

Jasper waved him off and headed toward the locker room. "See ya, Anton," Jasper said.

"Come on!" Anton called. "I'm not kidding!"

Jasper kept walking, his smile growing wider. But Anton was right. It had worked for him. He made a mental note to stop by Slate's office to thank her — and talk to her about Anton's request. After all, being back on the team was great.

ABOUT THE AUTHOR

Eric Stevens lives in St. Paul, Minnesota. He is studying to become a middle-school English teacher. Some of his favorite things include pizza, playing video games, watching cooking shows on TV, riding his bike, and trying new restaurants. Some of his least favorite things include olives and shoveling snow.

GLOSSARY

confident (KON-fuh-duhnt)—certain that things will happen in the way you want

discipline (DISS-uh-plin)—control over the way you or other people behave

opportunity (op-ur-TOO-nuh-tee)—a chance to do something

replacement (ri-PLAYSS-muhnt)—a thing or person put in place of another

reputation (rep-yuh-TAY-shuhn)—your worth or character, as judged by other people

request (ri-KWEST)—something that you ask for

scrimmage (SKRIM-ij)—a game played for practice in football and other sports

suspension (suh-SPEN-shuhn)—a punishment that involves stopping a person from taking part in an activity for a short while

DISCUSSION QUESTIONS

1. Do you think Charlie and Anton are good friends? Talk about why or why not.

2. Do you think Jasper made the right decision when he quit the football team after his mistake last season? Explain your answer.

3. Talk about Coach's decision to leave Kyle in Jasper's old positon. Do you think this was a fair choice? How would you have reacted if you were Jasper?

WRITING PROMPTS

1. Pretend you're Kyle. Write a paragraph about how you would feel when you found out Jasper rejoined the football team.

2. Were you surprised by Anton's request for help at the end? Write about what you would do if you were in Jasper's position.

3. Have you ever been forced to choose between two different groups of friends? Write about how you dealt with the situation. What did you do? How did you feel?

More About
FOOTBALL

OFFENSIVE POSITIONS INCLUDE:

QUARTERBACK — the leader of the team who calls plays, yells signals, and receives the ball from the center; this player also hands the ball off to a running back, throws to a receiver, or runs with it

CENTER — the player who snaps the ball to the quarterback

RUNNING BACK — a player who runs with the ball

FULLBACK — a player in charge of blocking for the running back

WIDE RECEIVER — a player who evades defenders and catches the ball

TIGHT END — a player who lines up to the left or right of the quarterback and acts as a receiver and a blocker

LEFT AND RIGHT GUARDS — the inner members of the offensive line who block for other players

LEFT AND RIGHT TACKLE — the outer two members of the offensive line

Football teams are made up of both offensive and defensive players. Only one group from a particular team is on the field at a time.

DEFENSIVE POSITIONS INCLUDE:

DEFENSIVE TACKLE — inner two members of the defensive line in charge of stopping running plays

DEFENSIVE END — outer two members of the defensive line in charge of holding the line of scrimmage

LINEBACKER — generally the best tacklers on a team who must often defend the run and the pass

SAFETY — these players are the last line of defense and must defend against deep passes and runs

CORNERBACK — players who line up on the wide parts of the field opposite the offensive receivers